dick bruna

miffy's birthday

World International

Little Miffy one fine day

was early out of bed

she washed herself from top to toe

there now, that's done, she said.

Then from her cupboard Miffy took

her very prettiest dress

but why? it was her birthday, so

she liked to look her best.

Then in came Miffy's mum and dad

happy returns! said they

and Miff said, thank you very much

this is a lovely day.

Oh look, you've made my chair look sweet

with flowers, just like my dress

with yellow hearts and little leaves

however did you guess?

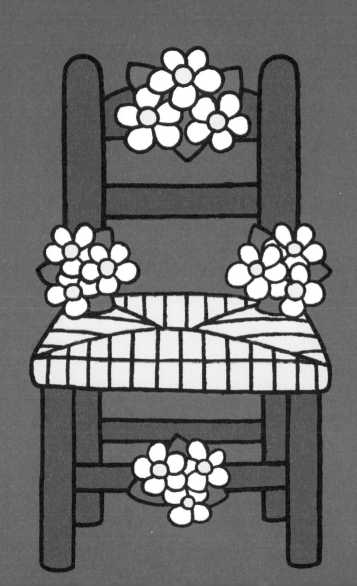

And what about those parcels there

are they all meant for me?

I must unwrap them straight away

oh, I can't wait to see.

Some scissors first that really cut

a lovely whistle too

and coloured crayons, oh hurrah!

red, yellow, green and blue.

Then in the afternoon her friends

Aggie and Win came by

a happy birthday, Miff, they said

and Miffy felt quite shy.

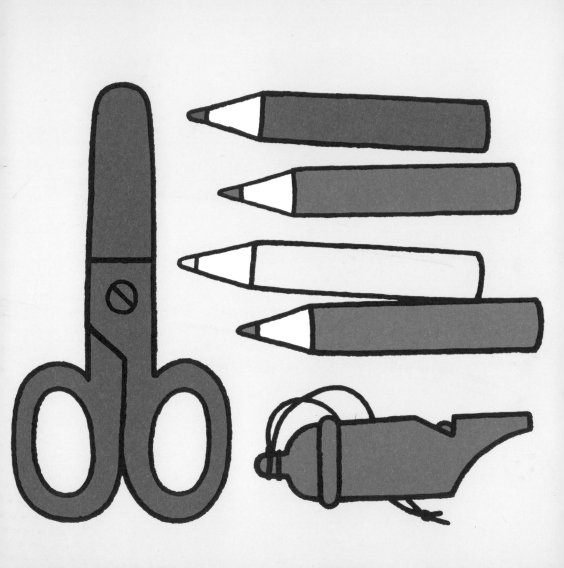

What fun they had, the three of them

they played some lovely games

and threw a shiny ball about

until the evening came.

And in the evening Grandpa Bun

and Grandma came to tea

and they had brought a parcel, too

whatever could it be?

A bear, a woolly teddy bear

so cuddly, soft and bright

I'll take him with me, Miffy cried

up to my bed tonight.

They had a real dinner then

Miffy at Grandpa's side

and Teddy sat on Miffy's lap

which filled the bear with pride.

When Miffy's mother late that night

took Miff and Ted to bed

oh thank you for a happy day

my birthday, Miffy said.

miffy's library

"het feest van nijntje"
Original text Dick Bruna 1988 © copyright Mercis Publishing BV.
Illustrations Dick Bruna © copyright Mercis BV 1988.
Published in Great Britain in 1997 by World International Ltd.,
Deanway Technology Centre, Wilmslow Road, Handforth, Cheshire SK9 3FB.
Original English translation © copyright Patricia Crampton 1996.
The moral right of the author has been asserted.
Publication licensed by Mercis Publishing BV, Amsterdam.
Printed by Sebald Sachsendruck Plauen, Germany. All rights reserved.
ISBN 0-7498-2982-6